Hannah Montana

One of a Kind

Adapted by Laurie McElroy

Based on the series created by Michael Poryes and Rich Correll & Barry O'Brien

Part One is based on the episode, "I Am Hannah, Hear Me Croak," Written by Michael Poryes

Part Two is based on the episode, "You Gotta *Not* Fight for Your Right to Party," Written by Steven James Meyer

DISNEY PRESS

New York

First Edition
1 3 5 7 9 10 8 6 4 2

Library of Congress Control Number 2008903367
ISBN 978-1-4231-1422-2

For more Disney Press fun, visit www.disneybooks.com
Visit DisneyChannel.com

PART ONE

Chapter One

Hannah Montana danced across the stage, singing the final chorus of "Life's What You Make It." She brought yet another powerhouse performance to an end with her strong, clear voice, and the crowd went wild, chanting, "We love you! We love you!"

"Thank you!" Hannah called out. "I love you, too!" She waved her microphone and blew kisses. "Good night, everybody!"

But her fans weren't ready to say good-bye. They started chanting her name. "Hannah! Hannah! Hannah!"

What a concert! thought Hannah. "You guys want more?" she called out. "Y'all are awesome!"

The crowd's chants grew even louder. "Hannah! Hannah!"

"I'll sing all night long if you want me to!" Hannah called back. She was having a great time. She didn't want the night to end either. She loved singing for her fans more than almost anything. After all, it was what being a pop star was all about! She turned to her band. "Let's kick it, guys!" she said.

The band played the first notes of "I Got Nerve." Then Hannah Montana's voice filled the concert arena, and her fans went crazy enjoying another hit-filled set.

The next morning, at a beach house in Malibu, Jackson Stewart was thinking about his sister's concert the night before.

"You want some toast," he sang, making up his own words to the tune of "I Got Nerve," as he and his dad made breakfast. *"I bet you do."*

"Please add some jam and but-ter, too," Mr. Stewart joined in.

"We're out of grape, so sad," Jackson sang. *"It's all your fault, you bad dad."*

Mr. Stewart stopped dancing. "You know what, son?" he said.

"Yeah, Dad?"

"You got nerve," Mr. Stewart teased.

Jackson laughed.

Just then, Miley Stewart appeared at the top of the stairs, bleary-eyed and still in her pajamas. Without her long, blond Hannah

Montana wig and her makeup, Miley looked just like any other high school girl. And that's exactly the way she wanted it. Only her family and closest friends knew that Miley Stewart and Hannah Montana were the same person. Miley loved being up onstage as Hannah Montana. She loved singing and dancing and rocking the house. But she loved her normal life, too.

Sometimes living a secret double life was exhausting. It was hard being a full-time high school student and a teen superstar at the same time. As much as Miley enjoyed being Hannah Montana, she wanted to make sure that people liked her for who she was and not because she was a pop star. So she lived her day-to-day life as average, brown-haired Miley Stewart and put on a blond wig and glittery clothes when it was time to transform herself into Hannah Montana.

It was the best of both worlds, just as her hit song said.

Her father, Robby Ray Stewart, started applauding as soon as he saw her. "There she is. Six encores. The voice that wouldn't stop."

"Well, they were such a great audi—" Miley paused and cleared her throat. Her voice was all hoarse and scratchy. "They were such a great—" That sounded even worse. "Whoa, this isn't good," she whispered.

"Here, take a sip of this," Mr. Stewart said, handing her a glass of orange juice.

Miley drank it quickly, sure the healthy liquid would change her croaky-frog voice back into that of a pop princess. She sang a line from one of her songs, practically choking.

Jackson cringed. Now his younger sister sounded even worse.

Miley turned to her father with a panicked expression. "Help me!" she croaked.

Later that morning, Miley leaned over a vaporizer, trying to relax and let the steam do its work.

"Do, re, mi, fa, soooooo . . ." Miley croaked. She threw up her hands in exasperation. ". . . not working!"

"And it won't if you keep talking," her father said, sitting down across from her. "You know, honey, this used to happen all the time to me when I was out on tour. And the only thing that got me better was when your mama made me not talk for a while."

"I can do that," Miley said, nodding. She'd do anything to get her voice back. The idea of not being able to sing was just too horrible!

Her father cocked his head. "*Mile*," he said.

"What?"

"You're talking."

"Dang!" Miley exclaimed. She had just spoken again. "Oh!" she groaned. And again! "Dang!"

She clapped her hands over her mouth. This was going to be hard!

"*There* you go," her father said. "Now listen, keep it like that or we're going to have to cancel that big concert on TV next Saturday."

Miley jumped up and waved her arms around as if to say, "No! No, please!" She *had* to do that concert! She ran over to the couch and sat yoga style, pretending to zip her lips closed, lock them shut, and throw away the key. She finished by throwing her arms out in a giant "ta-da!" motion.

Jackson had been watching. He went into the living room and handed his sister the whiteboard that usually hung on the wall in the kitchen. Normally, the family used it to leave each other notes and jot down grocery lists. Now it would serve as Miley's temporary "voice."

"That's our girl," Jackson said encouragingly. "Now if you want to say anything for the next few days, just use that. Hannah Montana has never cancelled a concert before, and she's not about to start now."

Miley eyed Jackson suspiciously. Since when did he care so much about Hannah Montana's concerts? she wondered.

Jackson didn't notice. "I know that would just break your heart," he went on, his voice thick with fake tears. "And when your heart breaks, baby sis, so does mine."

Yeah, right, Miley thought. She quickly

scribbled something on the dry-erase board, then handed it to her father with an irritated scowl.

Mr. Stewart read Miley's words out loud. "'You got a hot date for the concert, don't you, *Jerkson*?'"

Miley crossed her arms and glared at her brother with an "I know I'm right!" expression.

"Dad?" Jackson cried defensively.

"She wrote it," Mr. Stewart pointed out.

Jackson looked offended. "I can't believe you would think I'd be that selfish, to put my own—"

But Mr. Stewart also suspected that Jackson wasn't playing it straight. He cut him off with a question: "What's her name, son?"

Jackson sighed. "Jenny. And she's a total babe!" he admitted. "So put a cork in it, froggy," he went on, turning back to Miley. "I've got a lot riding on this."

Miley glared at her brother. Her throat had completely shut down on her and all Jackson could think about was his date? Typical!

Miley opened her mouth to yell.

"Ah—ah—ah," Jackson warned her, grinning. "Use the pad."

Miley took the whiteboard back from her father and whacked her brother on the arm with it.

He winced and turned to his father for support.

Mr. Stewart just smiled. "Couldn't have said it better myself," he teased.

Chapter Two

By the next afternoon, Miley's voice still hadn't gotten better, and she was even more nervous about missing Saturday's concert. Plus, the whole whiteboard thing was already starting to get old. Still, she tried to make herself feel better by hanging out at the beach with her best friend, Lilly Truscott. Lilly was one of only two people outside Miley's family who knew about her secret pop star identity. The two of them sat at a table in front of Rico's Snack Bar, a favorite hangout. Miley was sucking on a lollipop, while Lilly stared, a little disgusted, at the growing pile of sticks and wrappers in front of her friend.

"Miley, I know you want to get better, but sucking on those lollipops isn't going to do anything but rot your teeth," Lilly told her.

"Uh-uh," Miley mumbled, shaking her head.

"Uh-huh," Lilly said, nodding.

"Uh-uh!" Miley said again.

But Lilly wasn't about to take "uh-uh" for an answer. No one wanted to look at a pop star with black teeth, after all. She grabbed the lollipop stick and pulled.

"Miley, release," Lilly said as Miley clenched her jaw. She drew Miley to her feet, but Miley simply refused to let go.

"*Grrrrr!*" Miley growled, baring her teeth like a dog.

"All right," Lilly said. "You leave me no choice." She raised her free hand and wiggled her fingers. "Tickle, tickle, tickle," she said, aiming for Miley's side.

Miley opened her mouth in a silent, helpless laugh, and Lilly yanked the lollipop out victoriously.

"Hmmmf!" Miley grunted. Then she walked over to the snack bar for a bottle of water. Her other best friend, Oliver Oken, who knew all about Hannah Montana, too, was sitting at the counter.

"Wow, a week without talking," Oliver said when he saw her. "That's got to be tough for a *girl*. Now *guys*, we're different, we don't need to talk. I could not talk for a month, it wouldn't bother me at all."

Miley rolled her eyes as Oliver kept rambling, then she reached for her whiteboard.

Oliver barely noticed. "Now, girls just talk, talk, talk, talk, talk." He held up his hands and moved them as if they were talking to each other. "Hey, Sally, nice capris. Oh, I love your purse—"

Miley cut him off by handing him her board.

Oliver read it and frowned. "Oh, now that's just rude," he said.

"Look, Miley," Lilly said, putting her arm around her friend's shoulder, "I know this is going to be hard, but you have to stop fighting it. And don't worry, we're going to be right here for you until you get your voice back."

Just then a cute friend of Lilly's named Todd walked by with his surfboard. "Hey, Lilly, want to catch a few?" he called.

Lilly's eyes lit up, and her arm flew from Miley's shoulder.

"Oh, yeah!" she said, instantly running to follow him.

Miley couldn't believe it! She knew her best friend loved surfing—and cute guys like Todd, of course, too. But hadn't Lilly just promised to be there for her? To help her through this hard time?

Suddenly, though, Lilly realized what she had done. She turned around and apologetically pantomimed how much she wanted to go.

Miley rolled her eyes, but she understood. She nodded and pointed to the ocean.

"Thank you!" Lilly mouthed, then she hurried after Todd.

No, Miley thought, thank *you*, as she reached into her pocket for another lollipop. She popped it into her mouth and sank into a beach chair to enjoy it and a little peace and quiet.

Oliver sat down next to her and sighed.

"You know, this is nice," he said. "Just sitting here, enjoying the sun, the beach, the fresh air, that's the thing about nature, it's just so quiet and peaceful. Not like the constant noise you get in the city." He made a bunch of city noises—honking horns, car alarms, and sirens—to illustrate his point. Then he held his hands around his mouth like a megaphone. "Pull the vehicle over," he announced.

Sweet niblets! thought Miley. She'd never realized before just how much Oliver could talk, especially when he didn't have anyone to share the conversation with. He just went on and on and on—and on! She banged her forehead with the dry-erase board.

Oliver just thought she was agreeing with him about the city noises. "I know, it drives me crazy, too!" he said.

Thankfully, Miley was saved from any more of Oliver's painful monologue when Dex, another friend from school, stopped by to chat.

"Hey, Oliver," Dex called, waving.

"What up, Dex?"

Miley sat up a little straighter. Dex was totally cute and totally nice. For a while, she'd even hoped he might ask her out.

"Hi, Miley. Feelin' better?" he asked, flashing a warm, adorable smile.

Miley smiled back and kind of shrugged and let out a little squeak.

"Great. So, maybe, if you're not busy Friday night, we could go to the movies or something . . ." Dex asked shyly.

Miley smiled again, feeling her heart beat faster inside her, and she started to write her answer on her whiteboard. The answer was going to be yes, of course!

Before she could finish writing, Miley felt Oliver's hand fall on her shoulder. "I got this," he said softly. Then he turned to Dex. "In your dreams, Poindexter!"

Dex looked confused.

Miley was stunned.

"We're playing hard to get," Oliver whispered to her.

But Miley didn't want to play hard to get. She wanted to go to the movies with Dex! She flashed the boy a big smile as she pinched Oliver's arm.

"Ow!" he yelled. "Okay!" He got the picture. He turned back to Dex. "What she meant was, movies-shmovies, just plant one on her right now, big boy!"

Miley pinched Oliver again—even harder. That was *so* not what she wanted!

"Will you make up your mind?" Oliver

said, rubbing his arm. "We're sending Dex mixed signals."

"Uh, maybe another time," Dex said, quickly backing away from them.

Miley fell to her knees in the sand. *D-e-e-e-e-e-e-ex*, she mouthed. But no sound came out of her mouth, and Dex kept going.

The next day in school, Miley sat in Mr. Corelli's class with her whiteboard. While Oliver fought to stay awake and Lilly day-dreamed about catching waves with Todd, Miley looked longingly across the room at Dex. She wondered what he was thinking. Would he ask her out again? Or had Oliver ruined it for her forever?

"'Four score and seven years ago' is the beginning of what famous speech?" Mr. Corelli asked.

Miley eagerly raised her hand, along with several other students, and quickly began to write the answer on her dry-erase board. Behind her, Oliver had slid down in his seat, as usual, trying to escape from the teacher's view.

Mr. Corelli made a beeping noise as he pointed from one student to the next. "Finger, finger, on my hand, find the smartest in the land," he said. "Keep sliding, Oken," he called out to Oliver. "I can still see you."

Oliver grimaced and hoped Mr. Corelli's finger kept on moving.

Finally, it landed on Miley, to her delight. "Miley, make me smiley," he said.

Lilly turned and grabbed Miley's whiteboard. "I got this for you!" she said helpfully. "Miley's answer is"—she read Miley's board—"'the Bettysburg Address.'"

She looked up. "I think she means Betty Burg's address," she told Mr. Corelli.

Miley waved her arms to get Lilly's attention.

"Who's Betty Burg?" Lilly asked her.

Frustrated, Miley jabbed at the board. Couldn't Lilly see that that was a *G*? Gettysburg Address, she thought, pointing. *Gettysburg* Address!

But Lilly couldn't read her best friend's thoughts. "*What?* The only other thing on here is 'I heart Dex' and I'm not going to say *that* with him sitting right *there*." Lilly's face fell as she suddenly realized what she'd done. "Oops!" she said, cringing.

The entire class—including Dex—laughed, while Miley buried her face in her hands and wished she could disappear.

No doubt about it, this whole no-talking thing was an official disaster!

Chapter Three

For the rest of the week, Miley did everything she could to make her voice better. She drank tea and juice and gallons of water. She spent hours inhaling steam. And she never uttered a single word. Not one! Finally, on Saturday, it was time to try out her voice.

Miley sat at the kitchen table, surrounded by family and friends, drumming her fingers.

"Okay," Jackson said, checking his

watch. "It'll be one week in exactly three . . . two . . . one. Speak!"

Miley was frozen with dread. What if she still sounded like a frog? What if she couldn't sing on TV that night? What if her singing voice was gone forever?

"Darlin', I know you're scared," Mr. Stewart said gently. "But you've got to find out sooner or later."

Miley stared straight ahead. She didn't speak, or even move.

"Dad is right, Miles," Jackson said. "Miles?"

Miley kept staring straight ahead. She *couldn't* move!

"Oh, great! Now she can't hear either," Jackson groaned. "You're falling apart just when Jenny and I need you the most—that is so like you."

Her brother's self-centeredness snapped

Miley out of it, and she turned to glare at Jackson. "Would you shut it already?" she yelled. "I'm nervous enough and I don't know if I can talk." She stopped, realizing that she *was* talking. And her voice sounded great! She raised her arms like a gymnast who had just stuck a landing and gotten a perfect score. "I can talk!" she said.

Jackson jumped in the air and gave Oliver a high five. His date with Jenny was safe!

Lilly rushed forward to give her friend a big hug. "It's so great to hear your voice again!" she said.

Miley held Lilly at arm's length. She had been saving up these particular words for days now. "'I heart Dex'?" she said sarcastically.

Lilly winced. Suddenly Miley's voice *wasn't* what she wanted to hear. "But the last thing you want to do is overwork it," she said meekly.

"'Betty Burg's address'?" Miley went on.

Oliver laughed at Lilly's discomfort. "Oh, man, did you make her look dumb!"

Miley turned to him. Lilly wasn't the only one who'd made her look stupid this week, thank you very much. "'Plant one on her right now, big boy'?" she mimicked, hitting him on the arm.

"Oh, like you weren't thinking it!" Oliver said.

Mr. Stewart stopped them before things went too far. "Okay, now we know Miley can talk. Let's see if *Hannah* can sing," he said. He started to snap his fingers and sing the lyrics to "Life's What You Make It."

Lilly and Oliver snapped their fingers and joined in on the chorus.

Miley just listened for a moment, nervous

to even try. What if she couldn't sing anymore? It was great to have her regular life back, but what if her pop star life was over?

Tentatively, she sang a few words.

Slowly, a smile spread across her face. Her voice was back!

Her voice got stronger as Lilly and Oliver started dancing around.

Miley twirled Lilly around, and Oliver played the air guitar, sliding on his knees. Then Jackson grabbed the table that had mannequin legs with bright stockings and began to dance with it. Everybody stopped to stare at Jackson, but he didn't notice. He was pretending the table was Jenny.

"Oh, Jenny, isn't the concert wonderful?" he said to the table. "What's that?" He leaned in, pretending to listen.

Miley shook her head. Poor Jenny, she thought.

That night, Miley felt confident and strong. She took the stage dressed as Hannah Montana and filled the arena with her powerful, clear voice.

But then everything began to fall apart.

It was totally mortifying. The lyrics started to come out raspy and broken *again*! Still, Hannah Montana was a true professional. She didn't want to disappoint her fans. She tried to keep on singing. But it didn't work. Her voice sounded worse with each syllable. Finally, all she could do was stare at the audience in horror. Her voice was *gone* this time—completely gone!

The next morning, Miley's doctor made a house call. While Dr. Meyer checked her throat, she sat on the couch next to her father, hoping the doctor would say everything was going to be okay. But it seemed it wasn't that easy.

"I'm sorry, Miley," Dr. Meyer told her. "This problem is not going to go away on its own. If you ever want to sing again, I'm afraid you're going to need surgery."

Miley's jaw dropped. Surgery! Huh? Was he for real? Didn't that mean the hospital? And more doctors? And maybe even stitches? This was even scarier than croaking like a frog on national TV.

Mr. Stewart reached over and squeezed her hand. But all Miley could feel were the grim words sinking in. She couldn't believe it. Was this for real?

Chapter Four

"**S**urgery?" Miley croaked. The fear made her voice even raspier than it already was. "Really?"

"Trust me," Dr. Meyer said. "We're talking about a very minor operation. I could do it blindfolded."

Miley whimpered. Blindfolded? She did not want anyone with a scalpel coming near her in a blindfold.

The doctor shook his head. "I *won't*,"

he assured her. "I'm just saying that I could. Not that you'd know. You'll be out cold. Doesn't that make you feel better?"

Miley's eyes bulged. Out cold?

"It doesn't, does it?" the doctor realized. "I should stop now," he said.

Miley looked at him. "Ya think?"

"I'm sorry," the doctor told her. "I'm just trying to reassure you. This surgery is no big deal. One hour in my office and one week in recovery, and you'll be as good as new. Okay?"

Miley sighed. "Okay," she said.

Dr. Meyer stood and headed for the front door. "I mean, really, the chance of anything going wrong and you permanently losing your singing voice are one in a million."

Miley's jaw dropped.

"Oh, boy," Mr. Stewart sighed.

Miley jumped to her feet. "One in a million? But what if I'm that one?" she hoarsely cried.

"Aw, Doc, you were *this* close," her dad said, holding his index finger a millimeter from his thumb. It would be impossible to calm down Miley now.

"When I said one in a million, that was just a figure of speech," the doctor said quickly. He grinned and paused. "I haven't done nearly that many."

Miley sat down again and buried her face in her hands.

The doctor tried again to make her feel better. "Not that I haven't done a lot . . . because I have," he babbled on.

But that was enough for Mr. Stewart. He walked over and wearily showed the doctor the door.

Dr. Meyer nodded. "I'm going," he said.

Miley, meanwhile, was totally freaked out. "Daddy, there was a one-in-a-million chance you'd be a rock star and that happened. There was a one-in-a-million chance I'd be a pop star and that happened. Face it," she croaked, "this family is one-in-a-million central."

Miserable, she stormed toward the kitchen as her dad tried to calm her down.

"Hey, Miley," he said, "I really think you're overreacting. This guy is one of the best surgeons in the country."

"Yeah, Dad's right," said Jackson, who was eating a bowl of cereal at the counter. "Besides, what do you think is going to happen? Just as the surgery's about to start, a meteor hits a bus, the bus drives into a hot-dog stand, a giant neon wiener flies into a power line, the lights go off in the operating room, and you spend the rest of your life singing like Aunt Pearl after she swallowed that kazoo?" He coughed, then made a whirring sound in his throat in imitation. "Remember?"

Jackson had been trying to show Miley that her fears of surgery were unfounded. But his story had the opposite effect—it scared her.

"Oh, no!" she cried out hoarsely.

Miley spent the rest of the day in her room doing what she always did when she was this scared and confused. She pulled her notebook computer onto her lap and slipped in a DVD of old family movies. One of her favorites was of the Christmas when she was little. Her mother had still been alive, and one of the gifts Miley had gotten had completely changed her life.

"Here you go, Miley," Mr. Stewart had

said. "I want you to open this one next!"

Miley watched her six-year-old self unwrap a package while her parents looked on. They were all in their pajamas, sitting in front of a giant Christmas tree.

Miley ripped open the box and found a little pink guitar inside. "Yes!" she whooped, pumping her fist in the air. "Just what I wanted! Now I can be just like Daddy!"

She jumped to her feet and sang her first original song while she strummed the toy guitar. *"Rock, rock, rock! Yeah, yeah, yeah! Rock, rock, rock!"* She gave the song a big *"Oh, yeahhhhh!"* finish, before waving to her imaginary fans. "I love you, Tennessee! Good night. Drive careful!"

Her mom and dad cheered. Then Mrs. Stewart turned to Miley's dad. "You hear that, babe?" she said. "This little girl might just end up giving you a run for your money."

Mr. Stewart smiled at Miley proudly. "Well, maybe one day I'll have to just take you up onstage with me," he told her.

Miley watched her six-year-old self jump around excitedly as her parents shouted, "Encore! Encore!"

She strummed the guitar some more. *"Jingle bells! Jackson smells from fifty miles away!"* She waved a hand under her nose. "P.U.!"

Then suddenly the camera fell sideways to the floor.

"I'm going to get you, runt!" a voice like Jackson's, but a little higher, yelled. It was followed by the sound of bare feet chasing each other across the floor.

From where Jackson had dropped the camera, Miley could still see her dad in his funny old mullet haircut and her mom with her long, dark hair and pretty smile.

"Don't you just love Christmas?" Miley's mom said to her dad with a sigh.

So much had changed since that Christmas, Miley thought sadly. Her mother was gone. The family had left Tennessee for Malibu, California, and Hannah Montana had become a huge pop sensation. But would she stay that way? Miley wondered.

Just then, there was a knock on her bedroom door. Miley closed her computer and put it aside.

"Hey, Mile," said her dad, opening the door and coming in with a mug topped with whipped cream. "I made you a cup of my famous *loco* hot cocoa. With the little marshmallows so you don't choke-o."

He grinned as he sat down on the bed, but Miley was too scared to even smile.

"Choke-o. Choke-o," he repeated. "I'm going to keep saying it until you laugh." He nudged her. "Choke-o."

Miley looked at him. "Daddy, what if something happens and I can't be Hannah Montana anymore?"

"Well, then I'll guess you'll just have to pack your bags and get out," he teased.

Miley rolled her eyes and gave him a playful push.

"Baby, that's not going to happen," her father said gently. "Everything's going to be fine. The only thing you need to worry about is what flavor ice cream you're going to be scarfing down after it's over."

"How can you know that?" Miley asked.

"'Cause there's some things in life a daddy just knows," Mr. Stewart said. "I know the sun's going to come up in the morning. I know Uncle Earl's never going to be an underwear model."

Miley smiled.

"And I know your voice is going to be fine," her father finished, kissing Miley on the forehead. "You get some rest now, bud."

Miley put her mug down on the night-stand and snuggled under the covers. "Good night, Dad."

"'Night." Her father walked to the door and turned off the light before leaving. "Love you," he said.

"Love you," Miley answered.

She lay in the dark for a moment, worrying about everything that could go wrong in surgery the next day. But all the stress had worn her out. She looked at her mother's picture, took a deep breath, and closed her eyes.

Chapter Five

The next thing Miley knew, she was on her hands and knees in the kitchen, and her father was calling her name.

"Miley!" he yelled. "Where is that useless freeloader?"

Miley popped up from behind the oven. Her face was covered in dirt and grease, and her hair was a mess. She wore an old, stained apron. "Right here, Daddy," she said.

Mr. Stewart waved a pair of socks in the

air. "I thought I told you to iron these socks. You know how I like a nice crease in my hosiery."

"Sorry, but I'm still cleaning the oven," Miley explained.

Mr. Stewart took a closer look at her dirty face. "Wait a minute. What's that on the corner of your mouth? Have you been eating the burnt bits off the broiler pan again?"

"I'm sorry, Daddy," Miley said. "I'm just so hungry." She popped the burnt crumb into her mouth and chewed. "Mmm . . . month-old trout skin. My favorite."

Mr. Stewart shook his head in disgust. "Quit stuffing your face and get to ironing. Just because that surgery ruined your singing voice doesn't mean you can lie around here licking up trout drippings like the Queen of Sheba."

"But I *can* sing, Daddy. I've been practicing." Miley opened her mouth and got ready to belt out a song. As she sang, a vase shattered. A window broke. And the next-door neighbor's dog started howling. Her voice was squeakier and raspier than before the surgery.

Mr. Stewart grimaced and put a sock into Miley's mouth to make her stop.

"Don't ever do that again," he said firmly.

"Okay," Miley said, her voice muffled.

"Now there is only one person in this house who can sing, and we all know who that is," Mr. Stewart said.

At that, Jackson burst through the front door. Miley's eyes almost popped out of her head. He looked like a rock star! His normally short blond hair was almost waist length, kept out of his face by a navy blue bandanna. He wore leather-studded bracelets and supertight leopard-print pants, and worst of all, he could actually sing!

"Rock, rock, rock! Yeah, yeah, yeah! Yea-a-ah! Jingle bells! Miley smells from fifty miles awaaaay!" He belted out the modified words of Miley's very first song.

"Ladies and gentlemen," Mr. Stewart announced proudly. "Please welcome Bucky Kentucky!"

Jackson pretended to be standing onstage in a huge arena and took a bow. "Thank you! Thank you!"

Miley stepped forward with a confused expression. "But Jackson, you could never sing!" she said. "And Bucky Kentucky? That's the dumbest name I've heard."

"You're just jealous because you don't have a state that rhymes with your name anymore, little miss nobody," Jackson said with a sneer.

"Oh, please, like anyone would ever be a fan of Bucky Kentucky," she replied.

Just then Lilly and Oliver ran into the living room. They didn't even glance at Miley. They ran straight to Jackson.

"Oh, my gosh! Oh, my gosh!" Lilly breathed. She started jumping up and down. "It's Bucky Kentucky!"

Oliver was just as excited. "Dude, dude, dude, you rock!"

"I love you!" Lilly squealed.

"Guys, what are you doing?" Miley asked her friends. "It's just Jackson."

Oliver looked around at everything but Miley. "Did I just hear something?" he asked.

Lilly shrugged. "It sounded like a washed-up pop star."

Everyone laughed, except Miley.

"Let's go, kids, or we're going to be late

for Buck's big concert," Mr. Stewart said. "The limo's waiting."

"Ooh, ooh. Last one in is a Miley!" Jackson joked.

Everyone laughed again as they ran for the door.

Miley followed them with a wistful smile. When had she become a joke? She wanted to go to the concert, but they all ran off as if she wasn't even there. "Guys, what about me?" she called from the porch. "I should be going to the concert! I was Hannah Montana once! Please don't treat me like this! I have feelings. I'm not a piece of furniture." Then Miley looked down and saw that she actually was. Her bottom half had turned into the mannequin-legs table! "Okay, maybe I am," she whimpered.

Then Mr. Stewart walked back in. "Hang on, kids," he yelled. "I've just got to grab my keys and my wallet." He spotted them on the round blue table that now sat at Miley's waist. "Oh, there they are!"

"Daddy, what happened to me? I'm nothing but a table," Miley said, looking down at the tabletop around her waist and her brightly colored stockings.

"Oh, honey, you're much more than that," he said.

Miley smiled with relief. Maybe things weren't as bad as they seemed. Her father had even called her *honey*!

"You're also a coatrack," he finished.

Suddenly, Miley felt a long wooden pole running up her back. Coats and jackets covered her face. She pushed them back with a growl. "Sweet niblets!"

"We'd love to take you along, Miley, but you just have too many . . ." Mr. Stewart looked at the coats hanging in front of her face. "Hang-ups."

"Good one, Dad," Jackson yelled.

Mr. Stewart turned back to Miley with a satisfied smile. "See? I knew I was funny." Then he headed back to the car.

"No! Don't leave," Miley pleaded. "Somebody help me! Please!"

But there was nobody to hear her. The limo pulled away, and a red jacket fell over Miley's face. It all seemed hopeless.

Then she heard a voice call from inside the house: "Baby girl, you always did have the strangest dreams."

Miley turned toward the sound. "Mama?" she said.

Chapter Six

Miley hurried into the house to find her mother standing in the living room with a sweet smile on her face.

"Mom, is it you?" Miley whispered. She reached out to give her mother a hug, but it was hard with a table around her waist.

"Your daddy gave you some of his *loco* hot cocoa before bed again, didn't he?" Mrs. Stewart asked, shaking her head. "He knows what sugar does to you. I swear, when I'm finished here, I'm popping into one of his dreams, and he is going to get an earful." Mrs. Stewart took off her shawl and hung it from the coatrack over Miley's head.

Miley pushed the shawl away from her face. "Not helping!" she said.

"It's *your* dream, sweet pea," Mrs. Stewart reminded her. "If you don't like it, all you have to do is change it."

"It's not that easy," Miley said. But all of a sudden, the table and the coatrack were gone, and she had her own legs back. "Whoa, hey, maybe it was. Where were you when I was eating trout skin?" she asked. She was still wearing the dirty apron, but her voice sounded easy and normal.

Her mom smiled, took her by the hand, and led her to the steps in front of the piano.

"All right, baby girl, we both know you

didn't dream me here to ask me that," Mrs. Stewart said. She sat down and motioned for Miley to sit beside her. "Now why don't you tell me what's really on your mind?"

Miley took a deep breath. "I lost my voice," she admitted. "And if it doesn't come back, then . . . then . . ." She felt her throat get all tight as her eyes filled with hot tears. She couldn't even say it. If she couldn't be Hannah Montana anymore, would anyone care about Miley Stewart?

"Miley," her mom began. She didn't need to hear Miley's words. She knew her daughter well enough to see into her heart. "Do you really think if you're not Hannah Montana, you're no better than a piece of furniture?" She pointed to the legs table, now back in its usual spot. "Look at that thing. I swear there's nothing more dangerous than your daddy with a pocketful of cash at one of Uncle Earl's garage sales."

"Mom, if I can't sing, then I'm just . . . I'm just . . . Miley."

"And what in the world is wrong with that?" her mom asked. "I think 'just Miley' is pretty darn terrific. And I know that she's strong enough to handle anything."

"She is?" Miley asked.

"Heck, yeah! That's the way your daddy and I raised you."

Miley smiled, so glad her mother was in her dream.

"You're a wonderful girl, and that's why your friends love you so much."

"What friends?" Miley asked. She frowned as she remembered how Lilly and Oliver had abandoned her for Bucky Kentucky. "You saw how they treated me."

"Oh, for heaven's sake," Mrs. Stewart said. "Lilly, Oliver, get in here!"

Instantly, Lilly and Oliver appeared.

"If she wasn't Hannah Montana, would you still be her friends?" Mrs. Stewart asked them.

"Are you kidding?" Oliver said. "Of course we would."

Lilly nodded and sat down next to Miley. "Miley, you were my best friend way before I knew you were Hannah Montana."

"Then why did you just walk out on me?" Miley asked.

Lilly and Oliver looked at each other and then back at Miley.

"Duh!" they said together. "It's *your* dream."

Then Miley felt her mother's arm wrap warmly around her shoulders. "It was only scary because you're so worried about that surgery tomorrow."

"It's true, Miley," said Jackson, coming

into the room dressed in regular clothing. "In real life, I sing like a starving walrus."

He waited for someone to object. No one did — of course.

"Mom," he said, "this is where you say, 'Oh, no, you don't, honey.'"

"Oh, no, you don't, honey," Mrs. Stewart said with a grin. "Just a regular walrus. A cute, tone-deaf walrus."

"Thanks," Jackson said.

Lilly turned to Miley. "I like your mom. She's funny."

"She's pretty, too," Oliver added with a dreamy expression.

"That's it!" Miley said stiffly. Was Oliver crushing on her *mom*? "You're out of here."

Oliver frowned as he began moving robotically toward the door. "Hey, why am *I* leaving?" he protested. He looked down and tried to stop his feet, but they were moving all on their own. "This is not fair." He grabbed hold of the door and tried to pull himself back inside, but Miley's dream kept carrying him away.

Jackson watched him go, then turned to his sister. "The point is, whether you're Hannah Montana or just Miley, you're still going to be the annoying, obnoxious little sister . . . that I love."

"A-a-a-aw." Miley got up and wrapped her arms around her brother.

"Okay, you can wake up anytime now," Jackson said.

Miley grinned and hugged him harder. She rarely got a chance to hug Jackson when she was awake. "I ain't done yet," she told him.

Happily, Mrs. Stewart walked over to her daughter. "You see, no matter what happens to your voice, you've still got the most important thing a person can have . . . people who care about you."

"You're right, Mommy," Miley said, drawing Lilly to her, too.

"Ya think?" Mrs. Stewart said with a wink.

Miley felt as good about herself as she ever had—as Miley *or* Hannah!

"Oh, what the heck," she said. "Oliver, get back here."

"Thank you," Oliver said as he walked back over to join the group hug.

Miley was glad to be surrounded by the people she loved.

"You were loved before you were Hannah Montana," Miley's mom assured her, "and you'll be loved long after Hannah's on one of those 'Where Are They Now?' shows."

"I think you're confusing me with Dad," Miley said with a grin. She walked over and lovingly took her mother by the hand.

"Oh, I am not worried about you one bit," Mrs. Stewart said, pulling Miley into another hug.

Miley buried her face in her mother's shoulder and held her tight. "I miss your hugs, Mom," she said softly. Her voice was thick with tears.

"Oh, baby girl, they're never far away," Mrs. Stewart said, rubbing her daughter's back. "All you have to do is think about me." She kissed Miley on the forehead. "Now say good-bye to your friends and get some sleep."

Miley nodded and slowly walked back over to her friends. At the same time, her father appeared behind her mother. He put his arm around her waist. "You did good, honey," he told her.

Mrs. Stewart gazed at their daughter.

"You're doing a pretty good job yourself."
She turned. "Except for that hot chocolate
before bed."

Mr. Stewart winced. Ouch! He was
about to get a scolding. Gingerly, he
backed away. "Yeah, about that, I know
you used to tell me not to, but this was
a very emotional—Miley!" he hollered
suddenly. "You can wake up now."

"Robby Ray," Mrs. Stewart went on,
"how many times do I have to tell you—"

"Mile? Wakey, wakey!" Mr. Stewart called.

"And I can't believe you still have that
table," his wife continued, pointing to the
brightly colored legs. "No wonder the girl's
having nightmares."

"I'm sorry, darlin'. You know I always
was a pushover."

He smiled and Mrs. Stewart smiled back
and reached out for a hug. "That you were."

Miley watched her parents embrace with a huge smile on her face. Her mother might be gone, but it was good to know they could all still be together in her dreams.

A few days later, after Miley's surgery was over, she stood before her mother and tentatively sang one of her songs.

"Don't be scared, baby girl," Mrs. Stewart encouraged her. "The surgeon did a wonderful job. Your voice sounds better than ever."

Miley smiled and nodded as her voice grew a little stronger. She even did some of her onstage dance moves for her mother.

Then all of a sudden, someone wearing a fuzzy blue walrus suit, singing horribly, and playing air guitar joined them.

"Jackson, cut it out, boy," Miley complained.

Jackson took off his walrus head.

"Hey, it's *your* dream," he said.

Miley made a face and shook her head. "Not this time," she said.

"Well . . . if it's not your dream . . . and it's not mine, whose is it?" Jackson asked.

Mrs. Stewart laughed. "I think I know," she said.

Just then, Miley's dad woke up on the sofa in the living room with a start and eyed the cup of cocoa on the coffee table in front of him. "*Aaah!* Mama was right about that hot chocolate," he said. But it was too delicious to resist—he took a sip, giving himself a whipped-cream mustache, and turned on the TV.

Upstairs, Miley was sleeping peacefully. The next day, she knew, she'd wake up ready to take the world by storm as Hannah Montana. And no matter what happened, she would always be Miley.

PART TWO

Part One

"Now, if you want to say anything for the next few days, just use that," Jackson said.

"Don't worry," Lilly said, "we're going to be right here for you until you get your voice back."

Oliver turned to Dex. "In your dreams, Poindexter!"

"Okay," Jackson said, checking his watch. "It'll be one week in exactly three . . . two . . . one. Speak!"

"Surgery?" Miley croaked. The fear made her voice even raspier than it already was. "Really?"

"I have feelings. I'm not a piece of furniture." Then Miley looked down and saw that she actually was.

Miley smiled, so glad her mother was in her dream.

Miley was happy to be surrounded by the people
she loved.

Part Two

Miley had a major case of bed head.

Jackson took the towel off his hair. "What am I supposed to do about this?"

"It's my mirror, and I'll block it if I want to!"
Miley snapped.

"It's time for 'Dr. Phillbilly' to kick it up a notch,"
Mr. Stewart said.

The next thing Miley and Jackson knew, they were
dressed in giant sumo suits.

"This is never going to work," said "Jackson," taking
off his shower cap to reveal Oliver's dark hair.

**"Hey, two feet or two hundred feet," Miley said,
"you still didn't leave me."**

"What was I thinking?" Jackson said, joking.

Chapter One

Miley shuffled into her bathroom, half asleep. She trudged up to the sink and checked herself out in the mirror. Ugh! Sweet niblets! She had a major case of bed head. The rest of her didn't look too good, either. Then she cupped a hand over her mouth to check her breath. *Woo-whee!* she thought. That is some bad morning breath.

"We have got some serious work to do,

my friend," she told her reflection.

She had decorated her bathroom to look and feel like a spa, complete with rose petals floating in a bowl of water, so it wasn't a bad place to be . . . if she ignored the unearthly sound of Jackson singing in the shower in his own bathroom next door.

Miley turned on the faucet, ready to wash her face, but only a trickle of water came out of it. Jackson was hogging the water again. Like any amount of water would make him presentable, she thought.

"Yo, Jackson," Miley yelled, pounding her fist against the wall. "Get out of the shower! You're using up all the water."

"Too bad!" Jackson yelled back. "You snooze, you lose."

Miley silently fumed, then ran over and flushed her toilet.

"*Yeowww!*" Jackson screamed as his

shower went from hot to icy cold.

"Who's the loser now?" Miley taunted.

"Okay, sister! It's on!" Jackson called. He turned his faucets on full blast, leaving even less water for Miley.

But Miley wasn't about to give up. "Oh, yeah, and so is this!" she yelled as she turned the sink's faucet as high as it would go. "And *this* is on!" she said, turning on her shower.

"Oh, yeah!" Miley said with satisfaction, giving her toilet one more flush.

"Cold, cold, *cold*!" she could hear Jackson scream.

"Good!" she replied. And just to make her point, she flushed her toilet twice.

Then Miley heard what sounded a lot like a pipe bursting. The walls shook, perfume bottles toppled off the shelves, and all the faucets in her bathroom dried up.

"Not so good," she said under her breath.

A few seconds later, Jackson marched into her bathroom wearing his old, ratty bathrobe, his hair covered with shampoo bubbles. "How am I supposed to rinse and repeat?" he said, pointing to his hair.

"Here's your rinse." Miley picked up the bowl of water and rose petals and tossed it in Jackson's face. She gave him a big smile. "Do you want a repeat?"

Jackson glared at her. Then he took some bubbles and blew them into Miley's face.

Miley wasn't about to let him get away with that, however. She started to push him. Jackson shoved her back. Mr. Stewart finally arrived to break up the squabble.

A couple of hours later, Miley and Jackson were still in their pajamas while they waited for the plumber to finish. After her tussle with Jackson, Miley's bed head had reached epic proportions, while Jackson's soapy hair was wrapped in a towel.

Mr. Stewart put down his newspaper as the plumber came down the stairs.

"Good news. I got the girl's bathroom working and the boy's bathroom should be done in about three weeks," the plumber said.

"Three weeks?" Jackson exclaimed. "That's not good news."

"It is for me," the plumber said with a smile. He patted his rather round stomach and thought about how much money he'd make repairing the Stewarts' old pipes. "Now I can finally get that tummy tuck. And just in time for swimsuit season."

Mr. Stewart gave him a thumbs-up. "Chicks'll be digging that."

"Yes, they will!"

The plumber drove off, leaving Jackson to wonder how he would ever survive nearly a month without his own bathroom.

"Three weeks!" he moaned. "What am I supposed to do about this?" Jackson took the towel off his hair. It was standing straight up in spikes of hard, dried shampoo.

Miley smirked and patted his head. "Look for a carnival. You're finally tall enough to ride the bumper cars," she said.

"Ring! Ring! Hello?" Jackson held up his hand and pretended to answer a phone. "It's the bride of Frankenstein," he sneered, eyeing the tangled mess on Miley's own head. "She wants her hair back."

"That's it!" Mr. Stewart yelled. "I've heard just about enough."

"But it's her fault," Jackson whined.

"It's his fault!" Miley insisted.

"It's *both* your faults," Mr. Stewart said. "That's the reason why, until the bathroom gets fixed, you're both going to be sharing Miley's."

Sharing Miley's?

Miley looked at her father as if he were totally crazy. "Daddy, say *what*?" she asked.

"This is so unfair." Jackson said. "She started it."

Miley dismissed her brother with a wave of her hand.

"You know what?" Jackson continued. "We can get her a cat box. We can put it on the deck. Everybody wins!"

Miley rolled her eyes. If anyone had to use a cat box, it was her annoying brother.

"Jackson, I want you to go sit on the couch, think about what you're going to say next . . . and then, don't say it," Mr. Stewart said firmly.

Miley smiled at the fact that Jackson was getting scolded. Cat box, indeed.

Jackson opened his mouth to protest, but Mr. Stewart cut him off. "Think," he demanded, pointing to the couch. "Now go."

Miley watched Jackson throw himself on the couch in frustration, then turned to her father. "Why can't he just share your bathroom?" she asked.

"Because that would deny you two the wonderful opportunity to learn how to work together," her father said.

Then they both turned to see Jackson scratch at the soapsuds in his hair and shake them out onto the coffee table.

"Besides, let's face it," Mr. Stewart went on. "The boy's a pig."

Miley grimaced, but she knew all she could do was groan and hope that the next three weeks passed relatively quickly.

Chapter Two

Miley walked into what used to be her beautiful, dream-girl bathroom the next morning and recoiled in horror. It had been completely Jackson-fied! Dirty towels were draped over her claw-foot bathtub. Dirty clothes and even more towels hid her velvet-flocked shower curtain. Her shelves were loaded with shaving cream, raggedy toothbrushes, and cologne. Worst of all, Jackson had hung posters of cars and girls all over her lovely aqua walls.

"My eyes! What have you done to my bathroom?" Miley cried.

Jackson stood in front of the mirror wearing his old bathrobe and a blue shower cap. He was plucking his nose hairs. Gross!

"Just a little reorganization," Jackson said calmly. He pointed to some of his things. "My shaving stuff? Right in this fancy new holder."

Jackson had rigged something on one of her towel rods. He rested his dirty razor and an old can of shaving cream inside.

Miley's eyes nearly popped out of her head when she saw exactly what the holder was made from. "You're using one of my *bras*?" she yelled.

"Actually, I'm using *two* of your bras," Jackson said with a smirk. "The other one's holding my hair stuff." He pulled back the shower curtain to reveal another one of her bras suspended from the showerhead. It held a bottle of shampoo.

Miley could only stare as Jackson pulled it down and released it like a slingshot. The shampoo popped out, and he caught it in midair. "You could market these puppies," he told her. "You could call it the bra basket. Oh, the *bra*sket!" He chuckled. Then he turned back to the mirror and began plucking his nose hairs again.

Miley shook her head. "That cat box is looking better and better," she muttered. Then she realized exactly what Jackson was using to pluck his disgusting nose hairs. "Are those my good tweezers?" she gasped.

"Yep, and they work great," Jackson told Miley, clearly enjoying her discomfort.

"No!" Miley screamed. How could she ever touch them again? Her eyebrows would fall out in disgust.

"Oh!" Jackson plucked a large hair and examined it more closely. "Finally gotcha, Stan!"

"Stan? You *name* your nose hairs?" Miley asked, totally repulsed.

"Just the really tough ones," Jackson assured her.

He had to be kidding! But even if he was, Miley decided, something had to be done about Jackson and his braskets and his nose hairs and his ultragross, stinky towels. And soon!

Miley threw her head back and screamed as loud as she could, "Daddy!"

That afternoon, Miley donned a surgeon's mask and entered her bathroom again. She used her foot to lower the toilet seat. Then she started to pick up Jackson's filthy clothes and towels. Why hadn't she thought to bring rubber gloves?

She knelt down and reached for a towel, then noticed Jackson's robe hanging over the shower curtain. That *had* to go, she decided. So she reached up to pull it down, only to have it fall on her head, completely covering her face.

"*Ahhh!*" she screamed, flailing her arms. "Get it off, get it off! It burns. Get it off! It burns!"

Finally free, Miley yanked off the surgeon's mask and ran to the sink, eyes closed. She splashed cold water on her face to clear it of Jackson's cooties, then grabbed for a towel. She started to dry her face, then opened her eyes—just in time! It wasn't a towel she was holding at all. It was a pair of Jackson's underwear! And of course they were dirty!

Once again, all Miley could do was scream, "Daddy!"

The next morning, Miley stood at the sink brushing her teeth. Neither Jackson nor his stuff was anywhere in sight. Maybe it was all just a dream, she told herself. A very, very bad nightmare. But seconds later, it was all too real, as Jackson shuffled in, half asleep.

His bathrobe belt hit her, and she ignored him. Then he cleared his throat, and she ignored him again. But there was no way she could ignore what he did next.

He leaned over and spit a giant gob of phlegm into the very same sink she was brushing her teeth in.

"Gross!" Miley told him.

But Jackson ignored *her*. He found the toothpaste and squirted it directly onto his teeth. Then he licked the top of the tube clean, put the lid back on, and grabbed his toothbrush.

Miley tried not to react. Clearly, he was *trying* to gross her out, and she wasn't about to leave her bathroom—not even when he kept jabbing her with his elbow as he brushed. She jabbed him right back. She could go on as long as he could.

"Stop it, Jackson," she said finally. "I have to spit."

"Me, too!" Jackson insisted.

He leaned over to spit a half-second before Miley—leaving her mouthful of toothpaste to land in the middle of his neck.

"Oops!" Miley said, smiling. She was definitely enjoying her mistake.

Now it was Jackson's turn to throw his head back and holler, "Daddy!"

❊ ❊ ❊

After that, Mr. Stewart watched Miley and Jackson in the bathroom. And it seemed to help . . . a little.

"Jackson, may I please bother you for a comb?" Miley asked sweetly as they each dried their hair with a blow dryer.

"Of course," Jackson answered politely. "And it's no bother at all, sister dear."

Miley glanced at the mirror to see if Mr. Stewart was still watching them. He was. She smiled warmly. "Thank you," she said.

"That's more like it," Mr. Stewart said. "Now keep it up. I've got to apply my sculpting gel before I go all frizzy." He patted his own hair.

But the minute Mr. Stewart left, Miley tried to shove Jackson out of the way to get a better look in the mirror.

"Out of my way," Jackson said, jostling her back. "You're blocking the mirror!"

"It's my mirror, and I'll block it if I want to!" Miley snapped.

They stared at each other through narrowed, angry eyes, like two cowboys in a showdown. Then they raised their hair dryers and flipped them to high and tried to blow each other right out of the bathroom.

Unfortunately, the only thing they blew was a fuse . . . and within seconds, all the lights in the house.

"Sweet niblets!" Mr. Stewart yelled from his room across the hall. "Family meeting! Now!"

Miley and Jackson stared at each other. They were both speechless for a minute, but they soon got their voices back.

"This is all your fault!" they shouted at the same time. And they pushed and shoved each other all the way down the stairs.

Chapter Three

Miley and Jackson sat on the couch, waiting for Mr. Stewart to read them the riot act. So far he had been too angry to talk. He stared into a hand mirror. One half of his hair was perfectly sculpted. The rest was a frizzy mess. And they knew how important Mr. Stewart's hair was to him. They were definitely in trouble—big trouble.

"Look at this," he said, trying in vain to pat the frizzy side down. "It's a crime!

What am I supposed to do about this?"

Jackson tried to lighten the mood. "I'm thinking it's a hat day," he said.

He and Miley both tried not to laugh. His tone was serious, but Mr. Stewart's hair did look pretty funny.

"I'm thinking you don't want to know what I'm thinking," Mr. Stewart said.

Miley bit her lip, and Jackson slid down in his seat. "I'm thinking you're right," he said meekly.

Then their dad took a deep breath. "Let me tell you a story about my days in the band," Mr. Stewart said.

Miley and Jackson both groaned. If there was one thing they could agree on, it was that Mr. Stewart told *way* too many boring stories about his days in the band.

"We know, Dad," Miley said, beginning the old story before he could. "You had a backup singer named Celine Dionowitz—"

"You told her to shorten her last name," Jackson added.

"And the rest—" Miley began.

"Is history," Jackson finished.

"That is a true story!" Mr. Stewart declared. "But are we talking about that now? No. We're talking about the fact that you two can't learn to get along."

"She spit on my neck!" Jackson said.

"I almost wiped my face with his under-wear!" Miley added with a shudder.

Mr. Stewart didn't respond.

Didn't he know how truly horrifying that *was*? Miley wondered. "Daddy, I'm going to live with that for the rest of my life!"

Jackson rolled his eyes.

"Hush up. Now listen," Mr. Stewart said, intent on finishing his story. "The band and I lived on a bus for a year. Five guys, one bathroom, and someone always ate a little too much barbecue." He waved a hand in front of his nose so that Miley and Jackson would understand exactly what that meant. "You know how we fixed it?" he asked them.

"You opened all the windows?" Miley said.

"Yes, as a matter of fact we did," her father answered. "But we also learned to get along by seeing life through the other person's eyes."

Mr. Stewart got up and walked across the room. He grabbed two of the kitchen stools and set them up so that they faced each other. Then he turned back to Miley and Jackson. "And that's what you two are going to do."

"Oh, no," Jackson whispered to Miley. There was nothing worse than when Mr.

Stewart played amateur psychologist with his kids. "Here comes Dr. Phillbilly."

Sure enough, Miley and Jackson were soon seated face to face on the two stools, and Mr. Stewart was standing, arms crossed, between them.

"Now, Miley, you pretend to be Jackson," Mr. Stewart said. "And Jackson, you pretend to be Miley."

"Oh, sure," Miley said sarcastically. "Give *him* the good part."

"Gee, I only hope I can do it justice," Jackson said just as snidely. He stood next to his chair and mimicked his sister in a high, annoying voice. "Hi, I'm Miley," he began. "Now I'm Hannah. Now I'm Miley. I'm a real girl. I'm a pop star!"

He sat down again and turned to Miley matter-of-factly. "Your turn."

"My pleasure," Miley told him. There

was an angry glint in her eye. "Girls, cars, nose hairs!" she grunted. Then she stood and made the only kind of music Jackson was capable of making—arm farts—before imitating his typical reaction whenever he got angry. "Good day! I said good day, Daddy! Hoo!"

Mr. Stewart merely stared. Things were worse than he'd imagined—much worse, it seemed.

Miley sat back down on her stool with a big smile. "I don't know about you," she said to Jackson, "but I feel much, *much* better."

Mr. Stewart leaned forward. "All right, that's it! It's time for 'Dr. Phillbilly' to kick it up a notch."

The next thing Miley and Jackson knew, they were dressed in giant sumo suits. The suits Mr. Stewart gave them to wear had more padding than a department-store Santa Claus. Mr. Stewart moved all the furniture off the deck, then handed them each a helmet and two giant batons with padded ends.

Miley checked her reflection in the sliding-glass door. She looked like she weighed four hundred pounds!

"Now, the year Uncle Earl bought Aunt Pearl a mulch-maker for Valentine's Day, they had to go to a marriage counselor," Mr. Stewart explained.

"And he dressed them up like Oompa-Loompas?" Miley asked, thinking of the characters in *Charlie and the Chocolate Factory*.

"He said they needed a safe way to work out their anger so they could finally sit down and talk with each other," Mr. Stewart said.

Miley and Jackson both slipped their helmets, complete with face guards, over their heads. But Jackson was confused. "Dad, I thought you said violence is never the answer," he said.

"It's not," Mr. Stewart said. "But if this little exercise helps y'all get to a safe place of genuine love and communication, then whack away."

"I'm not hitting a girl," Jackson said.

"Good," Miley said, raising the baton over her head. "Then this should be fun!" She gave her brother a big wallop.

Jackson bounced against the deck's railing and hit the floor with a thump. He was well protected by his padding and his helmet, but his big round shape made it hard to get up. He rolled from side to side, finally using his baton to help him.

"Now you've done it. I'm so gonna . . ."

But Jackson didn't have time to finish. Miley swung her baton and whacked him to the ground again. "C'mon, butterball," she taunted, "is that the best you can—"

Whack! Jackson's baton flew out and knocked *her* across the floor.

"Waaaah!" Miley screamed as she landed with a bounce.

"Okay, are you guys ready to really sit down and talk?" Mr. Stewart asked them.

But Miley and Jackson didn't hear him. They were way too busy whacking!

"I guess not," Mr. Stewart said.

"Get off me, blubber butt!" Miley yelled.

"In your dreams, Hannah *Fat*ana!"

Mr. Stewart watched them roll around for a few minutes, then finally made them stop. He sighed as he helped them up. He'd have to try something else . . . something even more extreme.

Chapter Four

"**Y**ou two are hopeless," Mr. Stewart said after Miley and Jackson had finished fighting their way in through the back door. "If you're going to act like kids, I'm going to treat you like kids. You're both grounded."

"What?" Miley cried, desperately tripping forward. "Daddy, I've got Beyoncé's big party tonight. She told me Chris Brown totally wants to meet Hannah!" Miley had been looking forward to meeting the singer for months.

"Well, Chris is just *totally* going to have to wait," Mr. Stewart answered.

"Come on, Daddy," Miley said, though it was hard to make a case in such a silly-looking suit. "Can't you just ground *Miley*? *Hannah* didn't do anything."

"Oh, here it comes," Jackson said with a groan. "'I'm Miley, I'm Hannah, I'm Miley—'" he said in a high voice, swaying back and forth.

"Shut up!" Miley yelled. She bumped his springy stomach with hers.

Jackson bumped her right back. "You're not the only one who has a life," he told her. "Dad, I'm taking Siena to see Panic at the Disco." A hot date *and* a hot band. He wasn't going to miss that for the world!

"Siena Grace?" Mr. Stewart asked.

"Wow, she's a cutie." He patted Jackson on the back.

"I know." Jackson grinned.

"Too bad!" Mr. Stewart went on. "Nobody's going *anywhere* except me. I'm going upstairs to take a hot bath and try to remember the good old days before you two could talk!" He stormed upstairs, leaving Miley and Jackson speechless.

"Way to go, Jackson," Miley huffed after a moment. "Now I'm never going to meet—" She stopped short as she noticed the huge smile on Jackson's face. "Why are you smiling? We just got grounded."

"True," Jackson said. "But *I* just thought of a way to *un*-ground us. Now follow me."

She followed him to the stairs, where their huge round suits knocked into each other again. The next thing they knew, they were on their backs once more, arms and legs flailing like upside-down beetles.

Jackson kicked and helplessly rolled.

"I'm getting real tired of this," he groaned.

A couple of hours later, Miley stood at the sink brushing her teeth. She had a mud mask on her face, and her hair was wrapped in a towel. Jackson, in his robe and shower cap, stood next to her, applying shaving cream.

Mr. Stewart came to the door. "Heard all the quiet and I got nervous," he said. "Everything okay in here?"

Toothbrush in her mouth, Miley gave him a thumbs-up sign, while Jackson grunted, his razor poised.

"Y'all keep this up, and the grounding will be over before you know it," Mr. Stewart told them. He nodded approvingly, then closed the door as he left the room.

The bathroom filled with an audible sigh.

"This is never going to work," said "Jackson," taking off his shower cap to reveal Oliver's dark hair.

"Maybe not," said "Miley," straightening up and pulling off her towel. Underneath was the blond hair that could only belong to Lilly. She admired her purple face mask in the mirror. "But on the bright side, my pores are all tingly."

Meanwhile, the *real* Miley, dressed in her Hannah Montana pop-star clothes and wearing her long blond Hannah wig and makeup, bounced along next to the *real* Jackson in the front seat of a borrowed truck. She touched up her makeup, looking in the mirror on the visor.

Miley hated to admit it, but her brother's

plan to get them both out of the house was brilliant.

"Jackson, you're a genius. And my hero," she said begrudgingly. Then she brightened. "Until we get home. Then I hate you again."

"Right back at 'cha," Jackson said cheerfully. "And careful with the makeup. I promised Thor I wouldn't mess up his truck."

Thor was a friend of Jackson's who had just moved to Malibu from a dairy farm in the Midwest. He was less sophisticated than most of Jackson's friends—and even less than Jackson had been when the Stewarts moved to Malibu from Tennessee. Hayseed was probably the kindest description of Thor that Miley could come up with. But he was a nice hayseed.

But did Thor *really* make Jackson promise not to mess up his truck? Miley wondered. She looked around in disgust. How would he tell? She reached down and picked up something in a greasy wrapper. "Oh, yeah," she said sarcastically. "I'd hate to get blush on his half-eaten hoagie."

"Quit complaining. You know we couldn't take my car without tipping off Dad." Jackson paused to check out the sandwich. "And I call dibs," he said.

Miley cringed as her brother grabbed the sandwich and actually took a bite. Gross! "Oh, yeah, that Siena Grace is one lucky girl!" she joked. Then Miley turned to look out the window. Nothing seemed familiar. A heavy fog shrouded everything in mist.

"Jackson, are you sure we're going the right way?" she asked. "I have a feeling we missed our turn."

"There was no turn," Jackson told her. "I would've seen a turn."

"How can you see anything with this fog?" she argued. "Face it," she said, "we're lost."

"We're not lost," Jackson insisted. "We're just not there yet. Stop nagging me, woman!"

"I'm not nagging you," she snapped. Suddenly Miley spotted something through the fog. "Deer!" she hollered.

"Whatever you say, *honey*," Jackson said mockingly.

Miley pointed through the mist. "No, *deer*!" she cried again.

"Whoa!" Jackson quickly hit the brakes and turned to swerve away from the animal.

The truck skidded across the slick road and crashed through what felt like a solid wall of brush. Then, finally, it stopped.

"Nice going, Ricky Bobby," Miley said, comparing her brother to the inept race-car driver in the movie *Talladega Nights*. Her heart was racing, though, about a million beats per second. She tried to take a few deep breaths. "You could've driven us off a cliff!"

"But I didn't," Jackson said proudly, "because I have lightning reflexes and I am cool in a crunch." He casually leaned against the steering wheel. Suddenly the truck tipped, then teetered forward.

They *were* on the edge of a cliff!

"Daddy!" they both yelled at exactly the same time.

Cautiously, Jackson leaned back. So did Miley. The truck did the same thing. But it still teetered and tottered like a seesaw on a playground.

It seemed that if they leaned back, they could keep the truck from falling over the cliff's edge. But for how long?

Chapter Five

While Miley and Jackson balanced on the edge of a cliff, Lilly and Oliver laid low in Miley's and Jackson's bedrooms, trying to stay as far from Mr. Stewart as they could get.

Knock-knock.

A sudden rap on Miley's door made Lilly panic instantly. She tossed aside her magazine and dove under the covers. "Don't come in, Daddy," she called in the thickest

Southern accent she could muster. It was a poor imitation of Miley's Tennessee drawl. "I'm sicker than a possum in a . . . possum hospital . . . *y'all*."

"Relax, it's me," Oliver said, slipping in and closing the door behind him. "And by the way, if Mr. Stewart comes up, don't talk."

Lilly peeked out from under the covers. "What are you doing? We're supposed to stay in our rooms until they get back."

"I know, but . . . listen." Oliver looked down as a loud, grumbling roar sounded around them.

"Wow, their plumbing really is messed up," Lilly said.

"That's my *stomach*," Oliver explained. "I'm *starving*."

"Too bad," Lilly told him. She shrugged her shoulders and shook her head. "If we go downstairs, we might run into Mr. — "

"Hey, Mile?"

"Eeep!" Lilly squealed.

Mr. Stewart was right outside the door.

"What do we do?" Oliver whispered.

"Hide!" Lilly said.

She dove back underneath the covers, while Oliver tried to open the door to Miley's balcony. But it was locked. Then he did the only thing he could think of. He jumped onto the bed.

"Not here!" Lilly said. "Get out!"

She pushed Oliver off the bed, and he rolled underneath it just as the door opened.

"Dinner's on the table," Mr. Stewart said, walking in.

"Umph," Lilly grunted from deep under the covers.

"You all right, darlin'?" Mr. Stewart

asked. He walked over and sat down on the bed.

"Umph-uh," Lilly grunted again.

"Now, I know you're upset about not getting to go to that party," Mr. Stewart said gently. "But you've got to eat. So, I grilled up your favorites. Robby Ray's hot-eee-doggies!"

He tried to pull the covers down, but Lilly yanked them back over her head and held on tight.

"Not . . . hungry," Lilly choked, pretending to sob.

Then suddenly Oliver's stomach rumbled from under the bed.

"Really?" said Mr. Stewart. "You sure do sound hungry. How about I bring you up a little snack?"

"Uh-uh!" Lilly let out a loud groan.

"Hey darlin', ain't no sense lying up here

being sad," Mr. Stewart told her. "Remember what made you happy when you were a little girl?" He launched into an old song, clapping to the beat. *"Camptown ladies sing this song, doo-dah, doo* — Come on, darlin', you've got to doo-dah with your daddy!"

Lilly pretended to sob even harder, just wanting Miley's dad to go away. "Alone . . . now," she wailed. "Girl stuff . . . *y'all.*"

Mr. Stewart shook his head. "Okay. Well, if you get to feeling hungry, come on downstairs." He got to his feet and, as he did, stepped on Oliver's fingers.

"Aaah!" Oliver wailed in pain.

Mr. Stewart turned to the comforter-covered lump on the bed. "Really, honey, there'll be other parties," he said. Then he walked out of the room.

Oliver crawled out from under the bed

as soon as he heard the door close. "That's it!" he yelled at Lilly, his fingers still stiff and throbbing. "Next time he comes up, *you're* under the bed!"

Miley and Jackson, meanwhile, were still dangling over the cliff's edge, afraid to move.

"Honk for help," Miley suggested. "Honk for help!"

"I know I would have thought of that," Jackson said. He carefully moved his hand from the side of the steering wheel to the horn in the center. He pressed it gingerly, afraid that even the slightest pressure would tip them over. It didn't, but instead of a horn, they heard a cow's loud *moo*. Jackson shook his head. Figures a hayseed like Thor would rig his horn to moo.

"Great," Miley said. "Looks like the only

help we'll be getting is from a lonely bull. How far down *is* it?" she asked nervously.

"How should I know?" Jackson said.

"Well, look out the window," Miley urged.

Cautiously, Jackson stuck his head out of the window and tried to peer below the truck. But even that little movement made them start to tilt forward again.

"Not like that!" Miley screamed.

Jackson quickly leaned back and so did the truck, to their relief.

"I'm sorry I didn't bring my extendo-neck," Jackson snapped.

Miley took a deep breath, then very carefully opened her door. But that didn't work, either. The truck began to tip again, so she quickly sat back and closed the door.

Only then did Jackson notice the sliding window behind them. Maybe they could crawl through *that* and into the truck bed.

"Okay, this is all about weight distribution," he told Miley as he slowly slid the window open. "If we crawl out the back way, the truck won't tip."

"Okay, I'll go first," Miley said, unbuckling her seat belt.

"Whoa, whoa, whoa," Jackson said. "I should go first. I'm heavier."

"Yeah, but I'm faster," Miley told him, "so I'll be able to get to my party quicker."

Jackson stared at her, shocked. Did she really plan to *leave* him there?

"And, you know, come back with help for you," she finished quickly.

Miley started to climb out the window once again, but Jackson stopped her. "I can't believe how selfish you're being," he said.

"I'm not being selfish," Miley protested.

"I'm thinking of my millions of fans. They'd be crushed if I died."

"Hey, people would miss me, too!" Jackson said.

"Oh, please. Your teachers would throw a party," Miley replied. "Thor would be too upset about his truck, and trust me, I'll get Daddy through it." And with that, both she and Jackson made a move to scramble out.

"Whoa!" they both yelled as the truck swayed and shook.

Jackson and Miley immediately sat back, both holding their breath until they stopped teetering.

"Flip a coin?" Jackson asked finally.

"Good idea." Miley nodded.

Then, moving as little as possible, Jackson took a quarter out of his pocket and tossed it in the air.

"Heads," Miley said, watching him.

Jackson caught the coin and slapped it on the back of his hand. It was obvious that Miley had won by the look on his face. "Two out of three?" he asked hopefully.

"Sure, why not?" Miley said sarcastically. Then she went on, "Oh, that's right. Because that would be *stupid*." She turned around and crawled toward the truck's back window again. "Uh-oh," she moaned, stopping halfway through.

"What?" Jackson asked.

"My belt's caught," she groaned, trying to wiggle herself free. It didn't work.

"Just try to grab something and pull yourself through," Jackson suggested.

"I can't! There's nothing back here but this rubber fish." Miley picked up the thing to show her brother. It was only then that she realized the fish was actually real. Between the stink and the slimy feel, she thought she might be sick. "Oh, no, it's not rubber!" She threw the fish over her shoulder and it landed on the hood, sending them teetering again.

Jackson tried to push Miley through the window, but it was no use. She was completely and totally stuck. "Okay, I'm going to come around and pull you through," he finally said.

"What? *No!*" Miley yelled. What if it sent them over the edge?

"Don't worry. The weight of your big head will keep us balanced," he assured her.

Then, while Miley shut her eyes, preparing for the worst, Jackson slowly climbed out the driver's side window and began to make his way back. . . .

Chapter Six

At Miley's beach house, Oliver and Lilly were both starving, and the smell of Mr. Stewart's hot-eee-doggies drifting up the stairs was making their mouths water. Oliver was convinced that he would starve to death if he didn't eat soon, and the roar of his stomach had pretty much convinced Lilly, too.

"Okay," Lilly told Oliver as she climbed down the fire ladder out of Miley's room.

"I'll distract Mr. Stewart. You get the food."

"Right," Oliver said.

"Oh," she said, stopping, "only mustard on my eee-doggie. The yellow kind, not the fancy kind."

"Got it," Oliver said.

"But not too much," she whispered. "I don't want to overpower the dog." She thought for a moment, trying to cover all the bases. "Unless there's relish. That changes everything."

"Would you just *go*!" Oliver said. He threw a pillow out the window, trying to hurry her along.

"All right, fine. I'm going!"

As soon as Lilly was on the ground, Oliver raised the ladder. Then he stood at the top of the stairs, waiting for his part of the plan to begin.

Lilly rang the doorbell. As soon as Mr. Stewart left the kitchen to answer it, Oliver snuck down the stairs.

"Well, Lilly," Mr. Stewart said, opening the door. "This is a surprise. You know Miley's grounded."

"Oh, I know," Lilly said with a big smile. "I'm here to see *you*."

"Really?"

Behind him, Lilly could see Oliver creeping into the kitchen. "Oh, yeah, turns out my Uncle Will is a big Robby Ray fan, and I was wondering if I could get your autograph for him," she said.

"Sure," Mr. Stewart grinned. "Come on in. Let me just get a pen and—"

He started to turn, but Lilly quickly grabbed him.

"Whoa, slow down there, cowboy," Lilly said. "I'm way ahead of you." She pulled a pad and pen out of her back pocket and handed them to him.

"I brought Uncle Will's special autograph book," she explained.

Mr. Stewart took the pad and flipped through the pages curiously. "There's nothing in it," he said.

"That because you're his first. How special is that?" Lilly said brightly. She snuck a look over his shoulder to see Oliver slipping the hot-eee-doggies into rolls.

"Well, come on in while I sign it," Mr. Stewart told her.

But Lilly stopped him again. "But it's such a beautiful night," she said, taking a step back out the door. "Perfect autograph weather. Let's not spoil it."

Mr. Stewart shrugged. "All right," he said. "So should I make it out to 'Will' or 'Uncle Will'?"

"Actually, Uncle Will . . ." Lilly replied, realizing that neither choice would give Oliver enough time to finish making their hot dogs and get back upstairs. She'd have to drag this out more.

"Will . . . helm . . . von Kieran . . . Garden . . . State," she mumbled.

She caught a glimpse of Oliver squirting mustard on her hot dog.

"Not so much!" Lilly yelled. She winced and smiled at Mr. Stewart, who was eyeing her suspiciously. "Pressure on the pen," she finished lamely. "Wouldn't want to poke a hole in Uncle Willhelm von Kieran Garden State's special pad."

"Here you go, Lilly," Mr. Stewart finally said. He handed her the pad. "Why don't you read it and make sure it's okay?"

Lilly took the pad and read: "'Dear Lilly and Oliver'—" Her mouth fell open, and she looked up at Mr. Stewart, realizing he was on to them completely. "Oh, boy." She sighed.

"Keep going, it gets better," he said.

"'How dumb do y'all think I am? Love, Robby Ray.'" Lilly smiled sweetly and batted her eyelashes. "I like the 'love' part."

Meanwhile, behind them, Oliver had started to tiptoe toward the back door. He had one hot dog in his mouth and two more in his hands.

"Hey, Oliver," called Mr. Stewart, turning around.

Oliver froze. "Ummph-ummph."

"What's the matter, son? Eee-doggie got your tongue?"

Back at Thor's truck, Jackson had just managed to make his way into the truck bed and had jumped off to safety. "I'm out! I'm free!" he cried with relief.

"Jackson . . ." growled Miley, who was still wedged in the window. What? Was he just going to leave her there?

"Dang it." Jackson sighed. He climbed back into the truck bed and started to tug on Miley's arms. She didn't budge. Then a large bird landed behind her on the truck's hood. Jackson saw it and froze.

"What's wrong?" Miley asked.

"Nothing, nothing, it's just a bird," Jackson assured her. It was still on the hood, but the truck hadn't moved. "It's not like it's going to tip the truck. It's all good."

Then a whole flock of birds suddenly flew down and joined the first one, and this time the truck *did* move.

"Okay, *not* so good," Jackson gulped. Then he grabbed hold of Miley again and pulled with all his might.

"Jackson, it's not working!" Miley

yelled. He'd have to leave her, she knew, if he was going to save himself. "Just jump!" she told him.

"No way! I'm not leaving you here!" Jackson said.

"Don't be stupid!" Miley snapped.

"Don't argue with me! We're going to be okay. We just have to work together." Jackson watched in horror as *more* birds touched down, and the truck tilted forward even more. "And fast!" he finished.

"Okay, I'll suck in, you pull!" Miley said. She threw her arms around Jackson's neck.

"One, two, three, go!"

Miley sucked in her stomach and Jackson pulled as hard as he could, until Miley finally popped out of the window and landed in the truck bed.

With a heavy creak, the truck slowly leveled out.

"We did it!" Miley cheered.

"Now, let's get out of here!" Jackson said.

They jumped off the back of the truck, then turned to see the truck tip forward and tumble over the cliff.

They stood and held each other, realizing how close to death they had just come.

Then Miley realized something else.

"I didn't hear it crash," she said.

"Must have caught on something," said Jackson.

They took a few steps forward and peered over the edge of the cliff they'd just been dangling from. The back of Thor's truck was just inches away.

"Yeah, like the *ground*," Miley said. She grinned and slowly shook her head.

"Nice cliff," said Jackson. "What is that, like two feet?"

"Hey, two feet or two hundred feet," Miley said, "you still didn't leave me."

She reached out and gave her brother the biggest hug she'd given him in a long time, and Jackson hugged her back—for a second.

"Yeah, I know. What was I thinking?" he said, jokingly.

"Oh, shut up," Miley said, but her tone was warm, not angry.

When it came down to it, Jackson had risked his life to save his sister. That was pretty special—even if he did hog all the hot water.

"Well, I guess we should probably go look for help," Jackson told her.

"Yeah, let's go," Miley agreed. "The road's over this way." She pointed in one direction.

"No, Miles, it's this way," said Jackson, pointing in the other.

"No," she said, "it's *this* way."

Jackson frowned, then remembered their newfound love for each other. "You know what?" He stepped back and nodded. "Whatever you say."

Miley caught herself, too. "No, whatever *you* say," she said sweetly.

"I think this is going to be harder than we thought," Jackson said.

After all, old habits *were* hard to break.

"No it won't," Miley told him.

"Yes, it *will*," Jackson said.

The next morning, Mr. Stewart sat on the couch reading the newspaper. "All in all, last night turned out pretty well," he said. "Everybody's safe, and I think you finally learned the benefits of working together."

Miley, Jackson, Oliver, and Lilly were all in the kitchen. Each one had a toothbrush and was scrubbing a different section of the stove and the counters.

"Yeah."

"Right."

"Uh-huh."

"Sure, Dad. We learned our lesson," Miley grumbled.

But scrubbing was just one part of their punishment that day. Mr. Stewart soon launched into the other. . . .

"Camptown ladies sing this song," Mr. Stewart sang.

Miley, Lilly, Oliver, and Jackson rolled their eyes and sang the chorus: *"Doo-dah, doo-dah."*

"Camptown racetrack five miles long . . ." sang Mr. Stewart.

"Oh, the doo-dah day."

The kids' hearts were far from in it, but Mr. Stewart was having a blast. "I do love being a doo-dah daddy!" he exclaimed.

Put your hands together for the next Hannah Montana book . . .

Superstar Secrets

Adapted by M. C. King

Based on the series created by Michael Poryes and Rich Correll & Barry O'Brien

Based on the episode, "Achy Jakey Heart, Part One," Written by Douglas Lieblin

It wasn't often that Miley Stewart had a Saturday afternoon off. On weekends, there were concert dates, in-store promotional events, guest appearances on TV. It was one major drawback to being talented, fabulous, and internationally known.

On the rare occasion that Miley did get a weekend afternoon off, she really appreciated it. After a packed week featuring two pop quizzes in math, two oral reports, and the annual gym class dodgeballpalooza, she was beat—and also beaten up. (Dodgeball was not her sport, especially when she was playing against her nemeses, Ashley and Amber. Those girls didn't hold back!)

If Miley had been dating someone, she'd probably have called him. Maybe they'd have gone to the movies, or just chilled on a quiet section of the beach. But Miley hadn't been interested in anyone—at least not seriously—since Jake Ryan, her gorgeous blond classmate. And that was practically six months ago.

Jake was also famous—a star on TV— who'd seemed crazy full of himself at first. Miley had thought he was a jerk. But then, after Hannah Montana guest-starred on his show *Zombie High*, the two actually connected. Jake admitted that he had a crush on a girl at school: Miley! Then Miley started to realize that she had a crush on him, too, at which point the two *really* connected, as in kissed! It was an amazing *This-can't-really-be-happening—Time-just-stopped* kiss, after which Jake broke the news that he was going to Romania to shoot a movie for six months. He was leaving Miley in the dust—or at least the fine, warm Malibu sand.

Of course, Miley knew that Jake had to leave for work. Of all people, she should have understood. It was a giant movie role in the big-budget spectacular *Teen Gladiators and the Sword of Fire*; it would change the course of Jake's career. He couldn't turn it down. But as her wise aunt

Dolly once remarked: The brain under-
stands one thing, but the heart feels something else. And so, while Miley's brain
knew why Jake had to go, her heart still
hated him for it.

In the absence of a boyfriend, Miley's ideal
partner for a Regular Girl Saturday was
her best friend, Lilly Truscott. Lilly was
one of the few people who knew Miley's
secret identity. She understood how badly
Miley needed a break, and she arrived at
Rico's beachfront snack bar prepared for a
perfect, stress-free afternoon. She'd loaded
up her MP3 player with their favorite
music; she had two sets of headphones, a
ton of sunscreen, and a pile of the latest
fashion magazines. She'd also snuck in a
couple of celebrity tabloids—Lilly was a
sucker for gossip.

"Lilly, why do you read that tabloid trash?" Miley asked between sips of strawberry-pomegranate smoothie (the dance coach on her last tour had said that pomegranate juice was great for the complexion). "They're nothing but lies."

Lilly read aloud from the magazine: *"Hannah Montana looks fabulous. . . ."*

Oh, thought Miley, well, in that case! "With the occasional glimmer of truth," she quipped, looking over Lilly's shoulder. She needed to see which of her outfits had gotten props.

"You didn't let me finish." Lilly continued reading. *"Too bad she's really a guy!"*

Really a . . . huh?

"You gotta be kiddin'," Miley scoffed. She should have known. Those magazines would do anything to make a buck.

"I can't believe you didn't tell me," Lilly

kidded. "You've slept over at my house!" She gasped in mock horror.

Miley looked at the picture more closely. They'd even put a fake mustache on her! Funny, she thought, as she examined her doctored face, it didn't look all that bad.

"Uh-oh," said Lilly, turning to the next page.

"Let me guess?" Miley said, rolling her eyes. "It's another article about Jake Ryan, isn't it?" This was another reason she didn't like reading tabloids. Jake's star was on the rise, so these days he was all over the gossip pages.

Lilly's voice turned unexpectedly solemn. "It says his movie is done and he's back in town for the premiere."

It took a moment for Miley to absorb Lilly's words.

Jake was back . . .